Welcome to ALADDIN QUIX!

If you are looking for fast, fun-to-read stories with colorful characters, lots of kid-friendly humor, easy-to-follow action, entertaining story lines, and lively illustrations, then **ALADDIN QUIX** is for you!

But wait, there's more!

If you're also looking for stories with tables of contents; word lists; about-the-book questions; 64, 80, or 96 pages; short chapters; short paragraphs; and large fonts, then **ALADDIN QUIX** is *definitely* for you!

ALADDIN QUIX: The next step between ready to reads and longer, more challenging chapter books, for readers five to eight years old.

Read more ALADDIN QUIX books!

By Stephanie Calmenson

Our Principal Is a Frog!
Our Principal Is a Wolf!
Our Principal's in His Underwear!
Our Principal Breaks a Spell!

Fort Builders Inc.
By Dee Romito

Book 1: *The Birthday Castle*
Book 2: *Happy Tails Lodge*

A Miss Mallard Mystery
By Robert Quackenbush

Dig to Disaster
Texas Trail to Calamity
Express Train to Trouble
Stairway to Doom

Little Goddess Girls
By Joan Holub and Suzanne Williams

Book 1: *Athena & the Magic Land*
Book 2: *Persephone & the Giant Flowers*
Book 3: *Aphrodite & the Gold Apple*
Book 4: *Artemis & the Awesome Animals*

Mack Rhino, Private Eye

Book 1: *The Big Race Lace Case*
Book 2: *The Candy Caper Case*

FORT BUILDERS INC

BATTLE OF THE BLANKET FORTS

by Dee Romito

ALADDIN QUIX

New York London Toronto Sydney New Delhi

For my amazing agents, Uwe Stender and Brent Taylor.
Thank you for building stories with me.

ALADDIN QUIX
Simon & Schuster Children's Publishing Division
1230 Avenue of the Americas, New York, New York 10020
First Aladdin QUIX paperback edition May 2021
Text copyright © 2021 by Deanna Romito
Illustrations copyright © 2021 by Marta Kissi
Also available in an Aladdin QUIX hardcover edition.
All rights reserved, including the right of reproduction in whole or in part in any form.
ALADDIN and the related marks and colophon are
trademarks of Simon & Schuster, Inc.
For information about special discounts for bulk purchases, please contact
Simon & Schuster Special Sales at 1-866-506-1949 or business@simonandschuster.com.
The Simon & Schuster Speakers Bureau can bring authors to your live event. For
more information or to book an event contact the Simon & Schuster Speakers Bureau
at 1-866-248-3049 or visit our website at www.simonspeakers.com.
Cover designed by Karin Paprocki
Interior designed by Mike Rosamilia
The illustrations for this book were rendered digitally.
The text of this book was set in Archer Medium.
Manufactured in the United States of America 0421 OFF
2 4 6 8 10 9 7 5 3 1
Library of Congress Control Number 2020936853
ISBN 978-1-5344-5245-9 (hc)
ISBN 978-1-5344-5244-2 (pbk)
ISBN 978-1-5344-5246-6 (eBook)

Cast of Characters

Kiara Pal: The designer on the Fort Builders, Inc. team

Caleb Rivers: The organizer on the Fort Builders, Inc. team

Jax Crawford: The builder on the Fort Builders, Inc. team

Eddie Bell: The artist on the Fort Builders, Inc. team

Junie Wheeler: friend and neighbor of Jax, Caleb, and Eddie; friend of Kiara

Brinley: Kiara's friend

Kepler: Camp Firefly counselor

Finn: Brinley's brother

Minka: Camp Firefly counselor

Amina: Camp Firefly counselor; Eddie's cousin

Contents

Welcome to Camp!

Kiara Pal had been looking forward to sleepover camp at Camp Firefly all summer.

She slept over Nani's house all the time. And she loved it. But sleeping at your grandmother's is

not the same as three whole days
with your friends.

Caleb, Jax, and **Eddie** all lived
near Nani, and whenever Kiara was
there, they worked on their business together. Fort Builders, Inc. was

so much fun. She loved building forts for people. (And animals!)

But at camp, they weren't business owners. It was an official vacation.

Kiara and her parents waited in line to turn in paperwork. Then

they dropped off her bags in the cabin she'd be staying in. Soon all the parents headed home, and the kids were given a tour of the campground.

"Hi, guys!" shouted Kiara when she saw the boys.

"Kiara!" they all yelled back.

The Fort Builders team was together for the weekend.

"Are you all in the same cabin?" asked Kiara.

"Yup," answered Jax. "We asked to be."

"Who are your roommates?" Caleb asked Kiara.

She pulled a list out of her bag. "There are eight of us. But I only know a couple of the girls."

"Is Junie in your cabin?" asked Eddie.

Junie Wheeler lived on the boys' block.

"She is! And my friend from school," said Kiara. "But I haven't seen either of them yet."

The kids went to the main outdoor area. There were camp

counselors in sky-blue shirts and tan pants waiting for them.

Kiara saw her friend **Brinley** and called her over to sit next to her. She didn't see Junie in the crowd of kids.

A counselor with **Kepler** on his name tag clapped three times. The other counselors responded with six claps.

Kepler clapped once. They clapped twice.

"It's some kind of pattern," said Brinley.

Two claps. Four claps.

"You're right," said Kiara. "Also, I'm so excited for camp!" she whisper-shouted.

Five claps. Ten claps.

"Me too!" Brinley whisper-shouted back.

Kiara caught on to the pattern. When they did four claps, she responded with eight claps.

A few kids at a time joined in until everyone had figured out to double the number.

Kiara thought it was very cool that they'd done a math lesson without saying a word.

Finally, Kepler clapped once, and everyone responded with two claps.

When he had everyone's attention, they talked about the camp rules.

The rules were simple to remember:

1. Be kind.

2. Work together.

3. Have fun!

They went over the schedule and all the activities the campers could do. Camp Firefly had arts, cooking, sports, a ropes course, and even a water trampoline!

When it was time to choose the first activity, Kiara knew exactly what she wanted to do.

She and Brinley picked horse-back riding.

"You have to meet my friends from Nani's neighborhood," said Kiara. She led Brinley over to the boys.

"Brinley, meet Caleb, Jax, and Eddie," said Kiara. "Fort Builders crew, this is my friend Brinley."

"I think my brother is in your cabin," said Brinley. "His name is **Finn**."

Caleb had a good memory and knew every name on his cabin list. "Yeah, he is. Maybe he'll want to do rock climbing with us!"

Kiara's smile dropped. "Rock climbing? I was hoping you'd go horseback riding with us."

"No way," said Jax. "I've been waiting all year to go up that rock wall." He pointed to the big

climbing wall over by the tennis courts.

Kiara was not surprised. Jax would probably climb right to the top.

"Caleb, come riding with us," said Kiara. "It'll be fun." She didn't see the boys all that often and was excited to hang out with them at camp.

"Sorry," said Caleb. "Jax and I made a deal. I go rock climbing, and he'll do book club with me."

Kiara looked at Eddie. "Are you climbing too?" she asked.

"Nope. I'm doing the art class," said Eddie.

Kiara was disappointed, but she did have Brinley to do the activity with.

"Okay, but we have to meet up later," she said.

They all agreed and went in different directions.

"And no getting out of eating lunch together!" Kiara yelled across the yard. But she knew they'd all be there. Wouldn't they?

2

Kiara's Idea

Kiara was glad she'd signed up quickly for horseback riding. The line behind her had gotten really long.

She stroked her horse's mane as she rode along behind **Minka**, one of the counselors.

Kiara's horse was gentle and graceful as he walked along the path.

Kiara loved being with Brinley, but it was weird not to be building forts with Caleb and the team.

"Earth to Kiara!" yelled Brinley.

"Oh, sorry. Did you say something?" Kiara had totally missed whatever it was.

"We should decorate our cabin," said Brinley. "Wouldn't that be fun?"

"Yeah, sure." Kiara wasn't all that into decorating. She liked planning and designing things instead.

Her horse gave a quiet *neigh* as they continued along.

"We have cabin setup after

this," said Brinley. "We could do it then."

They still needed to meet the other girls and get settled in. They also had to pick their bunks and make their beds.

The horses came to a stop, and the camp counselors helped all the kids get down.

"You'll have a couple more chances to ride if you want to," said Minka. "Maybe I'll see you all back here tomorrow."

Kiara did love horseback riding,

but first she wanted to see what the boys would choose.

The kids all headed to their cabins.

Kiara ran right into Junie. Literally, right into her.

"Oops!" Junie stepped back. "Oh, hi, Kiara!"

"Hi, Junie." Kiara rubbed her head where they'd crashed into each other. "We're in the same cabin!"

"I know! I can't wait to decorate," said Junie.

There it was again with the decorating. Kiara wished she was as excited as the other girls, but she just wasn't.

The cabin was one big room with a bathroom at the end. There were four bunk beds—two on each side.

"I call the top bunk!" six of the

girls shouted. There were only four top bunks.

"I'll take a bottom bunk," said Kiara. She got her stuff from the pile and plopped it on one of the beds.

"I will too," said Brinley.

It was a standoff between the other girls. No one wanted to give in.

"Okay, okay," said Kiara. "How can everyone get what they want?" It was a question her teachers asked when kids disagreed.

"Well, there are only four top

bunks, and there are six of us," said one of the girls. "I don't think we *can* all get what we want."

She had a good point. But sometimes you have to think outside the box to find a solution.

"What if we switch each day?" suggested Junie.

"Good idea," said one of the other girls, "but then we'd be switching sheets every day."

"We could push the beds together," suggested another girl. "But I wouldn't want to be the one sleeping between the two mattresses."

The top bunk was something different. Something fun they couldn't do at home.

How could they make the bottom bunks just as fun?

Kiara looked around the room.

"I have an idea," she said. "What if the whole room was fun to sleep in?"

"What do you mean?" asked Junie.

"We could build a massive

blanket fort!" Kiara lifted her comforter in the air.

"That would be ah-maze-ing," said Brinley.

Soon everyone was talking at once. They were excited and full of ideas!

Kiara knew how to build forts. And she was pretty sure the girls would know how to build sleepover forts.

"I bet we could even win the camp's CREATE! award," said Brinley.

"What's that?" asked Junie.

"The camp awards this really cool trophy to the camper or the cabin that creates something incredible," answered Brinley. "It can be anything, but you have to make it from scratch with basic materials."

Now, *that* was something Kiara could get excited about.

"I love it!" said Kiara. If there was an award that was perfect for her, it was a CREATE! award. "Who's in?" she asked.

"ME!" they all shouted out loud. They threw their stuff on whichever bed was the closest. The top bunk **dilemma** had been solved.

Every bed would be awesome!

And their blanket fort might even win them the top prize!

3

Gather the Supplies

The girls scrambled to collect supplies. Luckily, they all had extra sheets and blankets.

"I usually put something heavy on the corners," said Junie. "But that won't work here."

"And I tuck the corners into something," said Brinley. "But there's nowhere to tuck them."

Kiara thought about all the forts they'd made. But blankets were very different from stacking boxes. She paced the room.

Back

and

forth.

Back and forth.

"We could use rubber bands," Kiara finally said.

"Rubber bands?" asked one of the girls. "How will those hold the blankets?"

"Ooh, we could wrap them around the tops of the posts!" Brinley chimed in.

"Right," said Kiara.

"We should look for some tape and binder clips, too," said Brinley.

Kiara could always count on

Brinley to think like a problem-solver. Plus, Brinley liked planning and building too.

"Brinley and I will see if the boys have anything we can use," said Kiara. "Why don't all of you ask girls in the other cabins?"

They all agreed on the plan.

The door to Caleb's cabin was open. Brinley and Kiara knocked anyway.

"Hello?" they said as they peeked inside.

No one was there.

"Hello?" they said again, just in case.

No answer.

"There aren't any activities going on right now," said Brinley. "Where are they?"

Jax and Eddie showed up.

"Hey, we were just looking for you," said Jax. "No one's in your cabin."

"Yeah, where'd everybody go?" asked Eddie.

"We were wondering the same thing," said Brinley.

"We were looking for supplies," said Jax. "Get this. We decided to build an epic blanket fort in our cabin!"

"Yeah, Caleb thinks we could win the CREATE! award!" said Eddie.

Kiara and Brinley gave each other a look.

"You guys cannot build a blanket fort," said Brinley.

Jax looked confused. "Why not?" he asked. "We're great at building forts."

"Because our cabin already decided to build one," said Kiara.

"And we want to win the CREATE! award," added Brinley.

They all stood quietly, not knowing what to say next.

"Well, we can both build forts," said Eddie. "There's nothing wrong with that."

"But we'd be **competitors**," said Kiara. "We're teammates, not competitors."

"It's just for fun," said Jax.

But it was more than that. There

was a prize on the line, and Kiara really wanted to win. Plus, there would only be so many building materials to go around.

She turned to Brinley. "We have to get supplies."

The girls ran to let their bunkmates know what was going on.

"You better not be looking for rubber bands!" Jax yelled.

The girls would have to be extra clever to pull this thing off.

But "extra clever" was Kiara's specialty.

The girls sat on their beds for their first cabin meeting.

They had gathered as many supplies as they could, but the boys had been searching for the same things.

"I bet Caleb already has a list of things to do," said Kiara.

Junie leaned forward. "Sure, but Caleb isn't the **design** expert on your Fort Builders team," she said. "That's you, Kiara."

Junie was right. Each team member played an important role in their business.

Caleb organized.

Kiara planned.

Jax built.

And Eddie decorated.

But when it came to **structure**,

Kiara was the one who could figure out the best way to build a fort.

Think, Kiara. Think, she thought to herself.

"I've got it! We could use string or rope. And clothespins if they have those around here," she said. "Broom handles. Or curtain rods. And chairs."

Junie took a journal out of her bag and wrote everything down.

"It would be great if we could find some lighting," said Brinley.

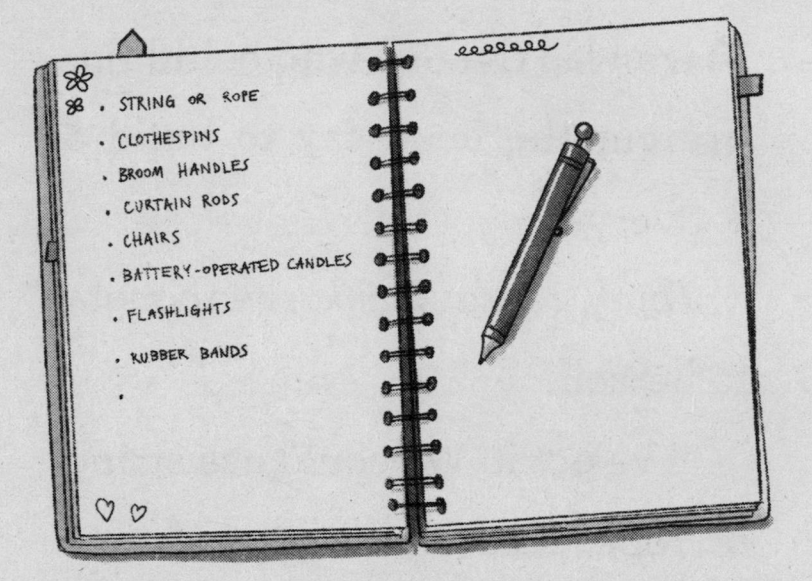

- STRING OR ROPE
- CLOTHESPINS
- BROOM HANDLES
- CURTAIN RODS
- CHAIRS
- BATTERY-OPERATED CANDLES
- FLASHLIGHTS
- RUBBER BANDS
-

"Battery-operated candles. Flashlights. Things like that."

Kiara nodded. "That's a good idea."

Brinley stood up and pointed in front of her. "This half of the room, find as much as you can on

Kiara's list. And this half can get the lighting."

Everyone got up, ready to get to work.

"Kiara, you're coming with me," said Brinley. "We have some trades to make."

Brinley grabbed a few of the supplies they'd already gathered and stuffed them into a bag.

"My brother can't resist a good deal," she said.

And off they went to **negotiate** for the Battle of the Blanket Forts.

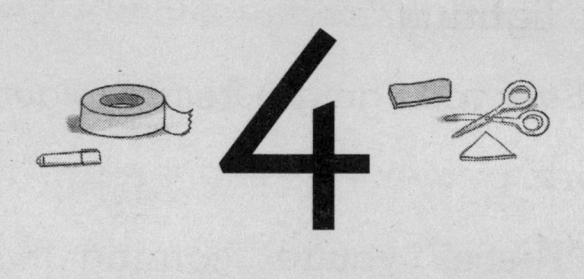

Fort Building!

Brinley and Finn went back and forth making trades.

"We'll give you ten binder clips for twenty rubber bands," said Brinley.

"No way," said Finn. "That's not an even trade."

"We'll need more rubber bands to secure the blankets," said Brinley.

But Finn disagreed. "We'll need more binder clips to secure the blankets," he said.

The swap went on for a while, but eventually, the girls left the cabin with some new supplies.

When they got back Kiara sketched out a plan, and assigned everyone a job to do. She was sure Caleb was doing the same thing.

The girls secured sheets to the bedposts on the top bunks with ribbon and clothespins. They stretched rope from one side of the room to the other. They draped bedding over the rope, making a sheet ceiling for their fort.

Kiara's purple sheets seemed to float above her. She loved the

Indian elephant in the middle with its detailed designs and pretty colors.

The girls saved the blankets for the bottom bunks. If those fell, at least they wouldn't take everything else down too.

They put chairs facing backward between the beds.

They secured the blankets to the chair posts.

They used every bit of supplies they had to make sure everything was sturdy and would stay put.

Brinley took charge of the lighting. She hung a string of lights in the middle of the blanket ceiling. She added battery-operated candles on each nightstand.

Junie decided where the extra pillows would go, placing them on the floor between each bunk bed.

They used the broomsticks to prop up the center of the blankets.

Finally, they laid the biggest blanket on the floor in the middle of the room.

The fort was like a circus tent,

but with all different patterns and colors.

"I don't care what the boys built," said Junie. "Our blanket fort is the best I've ever seen."

The other girls agreed.

"And we finished with ten minutes to spare before the next activity," said Brinley.

"Should we go on the playground to celebrate?" asked Kiara.

Without a word, they all got up, pushed aside the sheet doorway, and ran outside.

As soon as the girls got outside, the boys came running out of their cabin.

"Kiara! You have to see our fort!" shouted Jax.

"We should take a picture," said Caleb. "In case we decide to do blanket forts back home."

"Great idea!" said Eddie. "We can use it to show customers."

Kiara watched as the three of them made a plan for Fort Builders. She felt a little left out.

"You should take a picture of yours, too," said Jax. "I'm sure it's great."

Kiara smiled. "It really is," she said. "I'll make sure I get a good photo of it."

She couldn't resist taking a peek inside their cabin.

"Wow!" she said.

Brinley and Junie ran up behind her. "Wow!" they echoed.

The boys had done something different with their fort. Instead of looking like a circus tent, it looked like a blanket version of a hut.

There was a flat roof and flat sides.

There was a perfectly even doorway at the entrance.

It was amazing what they'd

done with the small space in their cabin.

"It's really great," she said. She was sure they'd win the CREATE! award for it.

All of a sudden there was yelling coming from the playground.

The group ran to see what was going on.

"We were here first," said one of the boys.

"There's no such thing," said one of the girls. "We all get to use the equipment!"

Their counselor Minka came over.

"Hey, hey, hey. Let's all cool down," said Minka. "You only have a few minutes of free time left. Don't waste it."

But no one listened. They were grabbing and pulling and running around.

Kiara didn't like it one bit. She walked away from the playground and sat on a large rock.

Caleb sat beside her. "This isn't so fun, huh?" he asked.

She shook her head.

"The rock climbing was pretty cool," said Caleb.

"Yeah, so was the horseback riding," Kiara responded.

"And my roommates are nice," he said.

Kiara smiled. "Mine too."

The counselors were still trying to calm everyone down.

"Maybe we should help," said Caleb.

Kiara nodded. "I'm sure they can handle it, but I have an idea." She grabbed Caleb's hand and pulled him up. "Come on. Let's go get things organized around here!"

"You had me at 'organized.'" Caleb laughed, and the two of them headed over to the playground.

5

Win-Win

Kiara pulled Minka aside.

"I know you're the counselor," said Kiara, "but I think we should have a meeting."

"Okay!" said Minka. "What do you think we should talk about?"

Kiara liked that Minka was asking for her input.

"Well, first of all, no one is following the rules," she said. "They're not being kind, no one's working together, and they're definitely not having fun."

Kiara liked rules. They were made for a reason.

"What should we do about it?" asked Minka.

"At my school we have a plan for things like this. There are three steps," said Kiara. "Can

I share it with the group?"

"I'd like that very much," said Minka.

By the time they were done talking, the other counselors had gotten everyone into a circle.

Minka clapped three times.

The rest of the group clapped six times.

That was enough to quiet every-one down.

"Thank you all for joining the meeting," said Minka. "Kiara would like to share some **strategies** with you that might help work out the problems you're having."

She turned to Kiara and smiled.

"At my school, we have a program called Win-Win," said Kiara. "There are three steps, and the goal is to find a solution that everyone can agree on."

Minka gave her a nod, so Kiara kept talking.

"First, you **identify** the problem," said Kiara.

Brinley raised her hand and waited to be called on. "The problem is that everyone wants the same equipment and the same playground space," she said.

"Does that sound like the problem?" Minka asked the group.

They all agreed it was.

"Next, you ask for solutions. Does anyone have one?" asked Kiara.

It took a minute, but kids finally raised their hands. They suggested things like taking turns, having time limits, and working out a plan before taking something that was supposed to be shared.

"Maybe we can sign up for things like we did with the activities," said Caleb.

"Plus, there are a lot of fun games we can play in the open space by the playground," said Jax. "I'll lead if you want."

One by one they gave solutions.

Before they knew it, everyone was smiling and working together.

"Great," said Kiara. "The last step is to agree. And it sounds like we've done that."

Everyone nodded as a chorus of "Yeah!" and "All right!" broke out in the circle.

"That's it," said Kiara. "Identify the problem, ask for solutions, and agree on the decision. We did it."

It didn't always work out that way, but it helped to at least start talking about it.

"How about some big Camp Firefly applause for Kiara?" said Minka.

The circle of kids got loud and then quiet in a matter of seconds.

"Moving forward," said Minka, "let's keep the camp rules in mind."

They said them together:

"*Be kind. Work together. Have fun!*"

Kiara felt good. She'd done something important.

Now, if she could only do it one more time.

6

Pies and Pancakes

After the meeting, there was another free-choice activity. Kiara signed up for baking with Eddie.

Someday he'd be on one of those kid baker championship shows. And he'd win for sure.

Eddie's cousin **Amina** was the counselor in charge of all the kitchen classes.

"So, amazing bakers run in your family?" asked Kiara.

"I guess so," said Eddie. "And Amina's even better than I am. But don't tell her I said that."

Kiara laughed. "My lips are sealed."

The class started with a big problem, though. They were missing **ingredients** for the pie they were supposed to make. And

Amina couldn't search for another recipe on her tablet because the internet was down.

Eddie stepped up. "I can throw something together," he said.

He searched through the spices. He checked the fridge. Then he wrote down a recipe and handed it to Amina.

"We may have to tinker with the temperatures and cooking times," said Eddie. "But I think this will work."

He even pointed out what had to go in the crust so it wouldn't break. He was a genius in the kitchen.

At the end of the class, Amina helped Eddie take two sweet potato pies out of the oven.

. . .

When it was lunchtime, Caleb, Eddie, and Jax all came over to sit with Kiara.

"I need your help with something," she said.

She explained what she wanted each of them to do. They were totally on board.

After lunch they gathered the two groups from the fort-building cabins together.

Caleb began the meeting. "First, we need to identify the problem," he said. "We all want to win the CREATE! award."

"Who has a solution to the problem?" asked Jax.

"I think the secret is in the camp rules," said Eddie.

"Be kind?" asked Brinley.

"No, but that's important too," Eddie responded.

"Have fun?" asked Finn.

"Nope, but that's also important," said Eddie.

"Work together!" shouted Junie.

Eddie nodded.

"What if we work together

and make our forts the best any-

one has ever seen?" asked Kiara.

"Together is better, right? We can

all win this thing."

They all shouted and cheered.

"So we agree?" she asked.

"Yes!" answered the group.

In no time at all they were

moving things from one fort to

the other.

The girls showed the boys how to make a reading corner with an umbrella. The boys shared their secret rubber band trick that held even heavy blankets up.

Brinley helped Finn string some lights in the boys' fort, and Caleb helped Junie organize the pillows so they'd be easier to lean on.

Eddie led a group that drew pictures. When they were finished, everyone exchanged their drawings and hung them on the walls.

When everything was done, the blanket forts looked AMAZING!

"There's one more thing," said Kiara. "Eddie has a really special treat for us."

The chocolaty scent escaped as soon as Eddie opened the container.

"Eddie's famous brownies!" shouted Jax.

Everyone took turns getting a chewy square.

"I made them at home yesterday,"

said Eddie. "Brownies are always better the next day."

They all agreed they were the best they'd ever tasted.

"Eddie can cook, too," said Kiara. "And because everyone worked so well together, he's agreed to show you how to make his famous pancakes tomorrow morning!" Kiara couldn't stop herself from jumping up and down.

"His pancakes are so good, you can eat them plain!" said Caleb.

He'd had more than his share of Eddie's pancakes.

"Would anyone want to learn that?" asked Eddie.

Everyone raised their hand in the air.

Eddie laughed. "Okay, then," he said. "I guess the Battle of the Pancakes is on!"

Kiara gave him a look.

"Totally kidding," he said. "No more battles. Just pancakes."

Everyone laughed as they reached for the brownies again.

. . .

The next morning Amina let Eddie lead the cooking class while she **supervised**.

He put all his ingredients on the counter. He wrote some numbers down on a piece of paper. He typed something on his tablet.

Kiara's grandmother had taught her to make some things too. (Her favorite was a super delicious rice pudding called kheer!) But she was also learning a lot from Eddie.

While Eddie finished preparing for his class on making the perfect pancake, Kiara filled out the CREATE! contest form.

But she didn't know what to put in the name box. There were too many people to list.

Kiara had an idea, but first she wanted to check with Caleb.

"You started Fort Builders, Inc., so I wouldn't use it without your permission," she said. "But what do you think about having another **division** of the company?"

Caleb got a big smile on his face.

"You mean like a new part of the company?" he asked.

"Yeah," she said. "If we need help or ideas, we can call them."

"I like it," said Caleb. "This new division should have a name."

Kiara had already thought about that.

"How about Fort Builders, Inc., Camp Firefly Division?" she asked.

"Ooh, I like that," said Caleb.

Kiara wrote it down inside the name box at the top of the contest form.

. . .

At the end of a fun weekend at Camp Firefly, all the campers gathered in a circle.

The counselors clapped four times.

The campers clapped eight.

"We hope you all had a wonderful time at camp," said Minka. "It's tradition at our last meeting to announce the winner of the CREATE! award."

"We were really impressed with all the entries," added Kepler. "You created some incredible things."

Minka continued. "And while we loved them all, one entry in particular really stood out."

"They have to be talking

about our forts," Jax whispered to Caleb. He was sure they'd get orders for blanket forts when they got back home.

"Not only was this entry a great example of using things like science, math, and problem-solving in the real world," said Kepler, "but it was also delicious!"

"Delicious?" Caleb whispered back to Jax.

Jax shrugged.

"Congratulations to Eddie Bell!" said Minka.

The kids went wild!

"I didn't even enter," he said to Kiara.

"I know," she said. "I entered you. Now go get your award!"

Eddie's smile grew bigger and bigger.

Amina handed him the trophy. "We saw you problem-solve, use your skills, *and* teach others. Plus, your food is so yummy!"

Everyone clapped and shouted. It was clear that they all agreed.

"Go, Eddie!" yelled Kiara and

the Fort Builders crew—including the Camp Firefly division.

She was happy to see Eddie up there with the trophy.

"But we have a little surprise," said Minka. "We noticed some incredible teamwork from one of the entries, so we've decided to give out a new award."

Kepler held up another trophy. "Congratulations to the Fort Builders, Inc., Camp Firefly Division for their teamwork and their fantastic forts!"

The team couldn't believe it. Not only had they won, but they'd inspired a new award, too!

Kiara and the team were beyond excited. Because sometimes, knowing your friends will always be there for you is the prize that really matters.

Word List

competitors (kuhm•PEH•tih•terz):
People who are competing; rivals

counselors (KOWN•seh•lerz):
Guides or assistants at a camp

design (dih•ZYNE): A sketch or
plan for a structure

dilemma (dih•LEHM•uh): A
difficult or puzzling problem

division (dih•VIH•jhun): A part
of a larger group

identify (eye•DEN•tih•fy): To
recognize what something is

ingredients (in•GREE•dee•ehnts):
Parts of a mixture

negotiate (neh•GO•shee•ayt):
To bargain with others

strategies (STRA•tuh•jeez):
Plans for reaching a certain goal

structure (STRUHK•shur):
Something that has been built

supervised (SOO•purr•vizd):
Oversaw a task

Questions

1. What three steps did Kiara use to solve conflicts or problems?

2. What supplies did the kids use to build their blanket forts? Have you ever built a blanket fort? If so, what materials did you use?

3. Which characters did nice things for other people? Why is it important to be kind?

STEM Activity

With the help of an adult . . .

Make Eddie's famous pancakes!

1 ¼ cups flour

2 tablespoons (tbsp.) sugar

2 teaspoons (tsp.) baking powder

½ teaspoon (tsp.) cinnamon

2 tablespoons (tbsp.) ground
   flaxseed

A pinch of salt

1 egg

1 ⅓ cups of milk

3 tablespoons (tbsp.) oil

1 teaspoon (tsp.) vanilla

Mix all dry ingredients in a bowl.

In a separate bowl, combine all wet ingredients, and mix with a fork or whisk until blended.

Add wet ingredient mix to dry ingredient mix. Stir with a fork or whisk just until combined.

Pour about ¼ cup of batter onto a hot nonstick pan, or a pan sprayed with cooking spray.

When you see bubbles, flip and cook until both sides are lightly browned.

*If you can't make Eddie's pancakes, go through the recipe and discuss the measurements used (What is a pinch?), the ingredients (What does baking powder do?), and the words used in the directions ("mix," "combine," "whisk," "blended").